A PENGUIN PUP FOR PINKERTON

STEVEN KELLOGG

DIAL BOOKS FOR YOUNG READERS NEW YORK

For Amy—
a perfect pitcher, pianist,
picture-book artist, and granddaughter—
with all my love

Published by Dial Books for Young Readers
A division of Penguin Putnam Inc.
345 Hudson Street, New York, New York 10014

Copyright © 2001 by Steven Kellogg
All rights reserved
Designed by Lily Malcom
Text set in Galliard
Printed in Hong Kong on acid-free paper
3 5 7 9 10 8 6 4 2

Library of Congress Cataloging-in-Publication Data
Kellogg, Steven.
A penguin pup for Pinkerton / Steven Kellogg.
p. cm.
Summary: After dreaming that he is the father of a penguin egg, Pinkerton
mistakes a football for a real egg, resulting in chaos all over town.
ISBN 0-8037-2536-1 (hardcover)
[1. Penguins—Fiction. 2. Dogs—Fiction. 3. Eggs—Fiction.] I. Title.
PZ7.K292 Pe 2001
[E]—dc21   00-030848

The full-color artwork was prepared using ink and
pencil line, watercolor washes, and acrylic paints.

Hi, Pinkerton and Rose. Hi, Mom and Granny. We learned about penguin eggs in school today. Did you know that in the Antarctic, a father emperor penguin cradles his egg on his feet?

He'll withstand cold and hunger for nine long weeks, because he knows that if his egg slips and touches the icy ground, the little chick inside will freeze.

When the eggs finally hatch, those little penguin chicks are the cutest birds in the world!
Their parents continue to keep them safe and warm until they're able to run around on their own.

Penguins are champion parents, but I bet *all* animals need something to care for and to love. Right now, Rose is probably dreaming about having a kitten of her own.

And Pinkerton is cradling that old football he found as if it were his egg.

Our teacher told us that a lonely animal will sometimes adopt and care for another animal. Once a gorilla adopted a kitten. Maybe Pinkerton could adopt and care for Rose.

I don't think Rose likes the idea.

Never mind, Pinkerton. I'll read a story to you and your egg.

Emily, look at poor Pinkerton. It's almost bedtime and he's still waiting patiently for his football to hatch.

Pinkerton, Granny says you're beginning to believe that you're an emperor penguin, and I think she's right.

Tomorrow I'll take you and your football to school for show and tell.

Class, we have an interesting visitor this afternoon. It seems that Emily's Great Dane has been inspired by our penguin unit, and he thinks his football is an egg. Do you have a question for our guest, Billy?

You bet I do! I'd like to know how this dog got *my* football that disappeared from *my* yard yesterday!

Hold on, Billy. I'm sure Pinkerton didn't know the football was yours. And now he thinks it's his egg.

Pinkerton believes he's an emperor penguin, and even when faced with blizzards or starvation, emperor penguins never abandon an egg.

Okay, pooch. You're faced with starvation. Here's a cookie.

As a penguin parent, Pinkerton is a *flop*!

Don't be sad, Pinkerton. Billy's football isn't really an egg. Let's walk home through the park. That will cheer you up.

Whoops. There's a football game going on.

Pinkerton, come back!

Get your dog off the field!

Police! Police! Arrest that beast!

Stop! You don't understand. Pinkerton thought they were kicking a penguin egg!

Ladies and gentlemen, a large dog has entered the game, taken control of the ball, and run for a touchdown!

Mom, Granny, help! Pinkerton stole a football from the stadium, and now he's tearing up a dog show, and the police are after him!

We'll be right there!

Pinkerton has disappeared. He's run away forever!

Come with me. I think I know where we'll find our penguin parent.

Yes, there he is! Out on the ice, cradling his egg and dreaming he's in the Antarctic.

THE RINK IS CLOSED TODAY

Hello, Pinkerton. Here's a little surprise that I've been working on for you. It's just about to hatch!

Granny, is it a Pinkerton chick or a penguin pup?

It's a baby Pinkwin for you and Pinkerton to care for and to love.

Come on, Pinkerton. Let's take our chick home where he'll be
warm and safe.